DIEGESES

D. HARLAN WILSON

DIEGESES

A DOUBLE

ANTI
OEDIPUS

FORT WAYNE, INDIANA

PRAISE FOR THE WORK OF D. HARLAN WILSON

Design & Layout by Matthew Revert
www.MatthewRevert.com

Cover Art © 2012 by Brett Weldele
www.BrettWeldele.com

Anti-Oedipus Press
Fort Wayne, IN

www.Anti-OedipusPress.com

TABLE OF CONTENTS

The Bureau of Me • 9
The Idaho Reality • 49

ALSO BY D. HARLAN WILSON

Novels
The Kyoto Man
Codename Prague
Dr. Identity, or, Farewell to Plaquedemia
Peckinpah: An Ultraviolent Romance
Blankety Blank: A Memoir of Vulgaria

Fiction Collections
They Had Goat Heads

Nonfiction/Criticism
Technologized Desire: Selfhood & the Body in Postcapitalist Science Fiction

For Lofton Gitt. And all of the (Big) Others.

THE BUREAU OF ME

"Arise, devour much flesh."
—Book of Daniel

ACT I

They marched into the office and announced that they were from the Bureau of Me. They wore black sunglasses and black suits and black ties. Stock g-men. They looked serious, eusocial, despite guestfriendly rictus grins.

"Me," intoned Curd, rolling the word around his mouth. "That sounds familiar."

Mz. Hennington cut them off. Maneuvering pointed sweaterbreasts, she lunged forward like a dogpoet and tried to take them out at the knees.

They dispatched her without incident.

Curd slipped his fingers around the glock taped beneath his desk, then killed a fly that landed on his desktop, smashing it with his free hand.

They removed their sunglasses. Affectedly. As if they were doing him a favor, or demonstrating that they possessed the efficacy to remove eyeware in a certain relaxed, levelheaded way.

They didn't have irises. Scarlet pupils marked the round white eyes.

Curd pulled the trigger.

Click.

"Shit. Shit."

One of them leaned over and placed a slip of paper on the desktop. He wasn't standing that close to the desk. Not within arm's reach, at least. In fact, he was on the other side of the room. Curd suspected an optical illusion. There were only two viable perps whose facilities might be responsible for the illusion.

Him. Or them.

Irresolute, he picked up the note and read it.

YOU HAVE BEEN CORDIALLY INVITED BY
THE BUREAU OF ME

He turned the note over. Blank on the backside.

"Invited where?" asked Curd. But they were gone.

• • •

That night, at his apartment, he rebandaged Mz. Hennington's wounds, then fucked her gently, from behind. Always from behind.

He came. He collapsed.

"I could use a cold beer."

He rolled out of bed and went to the kitchen and opened the refrigerator. It was empty.

The door closed like a flyleaf.

"You have been invited," said a seething, torpid voice. "Cordially."

Startled, Curd turned around and almost fell over, forgetting to move his feet. He made no effort to conceal the unburied carnival of his guyparts.

The man sat at the dinette table. He took a sip of beer, made a face, and tossed the bottle across the floor. It didn't break. Bleeding suds, it spun into a corner and clanked against a swell of empties.

"Invited where, dipshit?"

The man may have been one of the earlier visitors, only he had on a cape, and he blurred in and out of focus. It wasn't a misperception on Curd's part; the man's body produced the effekt. Out of focus, he looked like a mothman, sitting there with tattered, febrile wings loosely folded behind him.

The man stood and released an electric chirrup. He adjusted his collar, walked to the front door and opened it. "You will not be invited again." He added, "You drink [ur-word] beer."

He slammed the door behind him. The latch didn't catch; the door creaked open and a trapezoid of sodium light extended across the room from the corridor.

Mz. Hennington came out wearing Curd's signature velvet robe. It was much too big and heavy on her and looked like an animalskin rug that she had draped over her shoulders. A breast hung free. "Who was that?" she asked, knees buckling beneath the weight of the garment.

"Crepuscular shitbreather." Arms akimbo, Curd flexed his pectoral muscles. "Who else? The Bureau of Me."

• • •

Curd finished the drink and ordered another one. "I need to start taking existence more seriously," he said. "I need to start existing more . . . properly."

The bartender nodded. "Is there a proper way to exist?"

Curd finished the drink and ordered another one. "Yes. No. I meant to say I need to start existing, like, what's the word . . . better? Better."

The bartender nodded. "Is there a better way to exist?"

Curd finished the drink and ordered another one.

• • •

The city smelled like burnt hair, burnt oil, burnt iron. Machinery in ruins.

Whenever he got too drunk, he called his mother. Payphones were harder and harder to come by, but eventually he found one. He touched a thumbscreen. He encoded the number.

She answered.

"I'm drunk, mom," he told her.

"Where are you?" she asked.

"It doesn't matter. It doesn't matter."

"Ok."

They fell silent. A spinner thrummed by overhead.

"Fuckerrr!" bawled Curd.

"What happened?" said his mother.

He closed his eyes, compressed his lips. "Nothing. I gotta go."

"Ok. I love you."

He hung up the phone and hailed a smartcab.

• • •

"They say it's unwise to indulge simultaneously in plastic and icevapor. A man might develop a greater affinity for one or the other, and then what? Holocaust. The merger of affordable merchandise and untoward evil."

Curd changed the channel.

"When the entrails explode, we are reminded of the entrails. Seeing the world incites mnemonic inscription. Where would we be without the eyeballs? And the eyeballs are connected to the thinkballs. And the thinkballs are the proprietors of language. And the thinkballs must be greased like mystic engines so as to most effektively and fluidly unleash the slickest verbiage. This is in accordance with the laws of some genre science fiction and horror splatterfare. The metallic aftertaste of everyday life and arterial sprays of hemoglobin do not disqualify the—"

Curd changed the channel.

A smiling [ur-word]. Spitting image of his high school geometry teacher, aside from the cavity in his neck that exposed the striations, the cables, the strings. The mutant epiglottis . . .

The [ur-word] nodded perfunctorily.

Curd belched.

"Look behind you," said the [ur-word].

His head turned on a pebbled axis.

There was a man in a flak jacket chewing gum with pointed conviction, as if he had invented gum that morning and was still riding the high. Red pupils danced out-of-synch across expansive eyewhites. Curd said, "Can't you dumbasses take a hint? I don't wanna come to your god-damned party."

The man collected him in a sack.

Curd didn't go down easy. He ran around the place for awhile, slamming into walls and pictures and appliances while screaming out lines from trashy pulp B-movies, passing them off as his own. But the man was stronger and faster than Curd. Not a fair fight. But a fair outcome, given the constituency of the players.

Quadrifoil jabs, scripts, perforations.

Smell of primevality . . .

Somebody beat him with something, somewhere, maybe in the trunk of a car, maybe somewhere else. He had to swallow his blood for a long time. He got used to it.

"This is how things progress," a voice said. "You start in one territory. Then you move to another territory, and you grow. And the people who gladrag you grow. That is progression, [ur-word]. Growth at every starpoint on the constellation of eternity. It is a simple process."

Thud.

Time passed.

Then they unzipped the sack and took Curd out and blindfolded him and tied him to a metal chair.

"I need to call my secretary," he said.

"Secretaries belie the cult of little men."

"I need to call my mom then," he said. "I feel like hell and I'm still shitfaced."

"You are sober as a stone god."

Curd tried to stand, to break free. No strength. He had been tied loosely too. He was disappointed in himself. "I don't deserve it, but everybody gets one phone call. Lend me the arm of common courtesy."

Somebody punched him in the nose. He tipped over backwards. Somebody kicked him in the ribs. Somebody else kicked him in the chin and he heard either a toe or his chin crack. Curd concluded it was the toe.

Rainmade curses and echoic hopfrogs followed him into unconsciousness.

• • •

He awoke sitting in an upright position, neck straight, locked into place.

Effluvial light shone through a window beside the table. He blinked.

He had been served a plate of sunnysideup eggs and raw white bacon garnished with a rotten sprout of parsley. There was also a small glass of orange juice atop which had been placed a folded slip of paper. Sans utensils.

Without thinking, he picked up a strip of bacon by the tail, tilted back his head, and slurped it into his mouth like an escargot. It hurt to chew—stabs of pain riddled his jawpiece. He spit the bacon onto the plate, confused and horrified that he had attempted to manhandle it.

The room had red walls and smelled of fresh paint. Empty, aside from the table. There wasn't even a door.

The scene outside the window looked more like a CGI landscape than a real vista. It might have been. A kind of prairie or savannah rolled away from his vantage point in every foreseeable direction, extending to the horizon. He spotted a few blue tarns and swamplike regions, and he saw a distant knoll or fell, but for the most part it was all grass and reeds bending in a diplomatic breeze.

Curd tried to open the window. It wouldn't budge. He put his ear against the window. Dull fizzing sound. The ear grew cold. Hair stood on end.

Tentatively he opened the slip of paper. It read:

EATING PIGMEAT IS BAD FOR YOU

He crumpled the note and threw it aside.

Squawking, he swiped the plate of food and the orange juice from the table and they smashed against a wall.

Growling, he lifted the chair over his head and slammed it against the floor. He dropped pistonlike elbows and fists upon the chair until it broke apart.

Crying out, he flipped over the table and kicked off its legs. He used one of the legs to bash holes in the walls. Clouds and flakes of plaster sifted across the room.

And then he screamed, a real scream, a true and un-bridled scream, full-throttle, neck swelling into a trunk of purple tightropes. Blood vessels popped on the skin beneath his eyes. He slashed the air, reveling in cutting noises that weren't there.

Curd waited for the tantrum to subside before throwing himself through the window. Daymares of rhymed poetry pageturned across his [über-word] as he fell, fell, fell . . .

• • •

. . . and landed on a dark, wet street. He fell on his side and knocked his head against the asphalt. Dizzy, he struggled to bring the world into focus . . .

He rebuilt the world with calculated squints of acuity.

• • •

"This is a bad one, Mom," Curd spit into the phone, wiping cold bangs from his eyes. It had been raining all night. He felt like it had been raining his whole life. He recognized the melodrama in his emotional core. And he milked the core like a snapaxle.

Static. Raindrops.

"Mom? Are you there?"

"Yes, honey. I'm here."

"I'm hurt."

"Really? How so?"

"I hurt my soul. My soul hurts."

"The soul is disconnected from the body. It's inside the body, but it does its own thing. Anyway you can't feel it. It must be something else."

"Like what? My aorta?"

"I'm not sure. Maybe. Unlikely, though. We can't really feel our internal organs. They're in there. But they do their own thing too."

"Ok. I gotta go."

"Be careful now. Try not to drink so much."

"I always do. Try, I mean."

"Good. I love you."

He hung up the phone and hailed a smartcab.

• • •

Despite extensive wounds, sores, bruises, and a sprained ankle, he forced himself to fuck Mz. Hennington. No foreplay. No lube. She looked at him over her shoulder, gazing purposefully into his eyes, as he stared at her ass and conjured images of medieval orgies and cheering crowds.

He couldn't come.

"It's all right," said Mz. Hennington, the sinewy knobs of her spine accentuated by the room's warm, nec-romantic blacklights.

"I know," Curd said coolly. "I've come before. I'll come again."

"I know you will. Let's try later."

They slumped onto their backs and stared at the ceiling. They listened to the soft revolution of fanblades overhead. Curd lost himself in the intricacies of the ap-paratus's spinning turbine. Mz. Hennington reached over and took him by the hand.

They locked fingers and fell asleep.

INTERMISSION

A pulsing, mirrored sphere hovered above the spires and smokestacks of the city like a Bad Idea. A wide holographic ribbon moved diagonally across its girth, showing the world its name:

THE BUREAU OF ME

Long tendrils hung down from the base of the sphere like roots, as if it were an eyeball that had been yanked from a socket and pinned to the pewter corkboard of sky. Lightning raced up and down the tendrils while a glowing, viscous substance fell from their tips in hulking globs that exploded onto rooftops and streets, constantly imperiling traffic and insulting the architecture of reality.

The Bureau of Me never remained in one place or one timescape. It drifted across the halfbaked firmament like an unmanned dirigible.

Within the sphere, a swarm of dark stickfigures moved across planks, up and down stairways, through an obstacle course of cryptic, technologized appliances with antlike speed and precision. This activity slowed and accelerated at unidentifiable intervals, but it never stopped altogether, and it never spiraled out of control.

Amid the finetuned tempest, the systematic bustle, centered like the eye of a hurricane, or the nucleus of an atom whose electrons have gone rogue, a man on a superscreen, peacefully freezeframed . . .

The man discharged an aura.

Not a glow—if anything it was a darkness, a kind of blot—but a signifier, a Magellanic signifier—as if shrouded in a filigreed metaphor that could be touched, grasped, physically experienced—as if the rays of history beamed from the straightedges of his cogworn flesh. Confronted with the spectacle of his presence, even the idle viewer couldn't deny the simultaneous visions of heaven, hell, and nothingness that deathdanced like sugarplums in their heads. He might have held the promise of Futurity in one hand, Armageddon in the other.

The footage was shot from a gutterhole as the man ambled down a sidewalk at dusk, fingers resting in the pockets of a black trenchcoat, head faintly downturned, shoulders pushed back. Above him, the cartoon sky. Beneath him, a short string of text that hastened across

D. Harlan Wilson

the screen. The text pulsed with light, cast there from his frame like a shadow of meaning.

ACT II

It smelled like shit. No, something else. Roadkill. A corpse. An old corpse, one that's been decomposing and rotting for months. Otherworldly stench. Beyond swinefunk. Impossible for the senses to negotiate. It hit Curd in waves as he neared his office in a vociferous flow of foot traffic. Dryheaving, he looked around to see if there was a culprit, a dead elephant, an exploded sewage pump, something. Something big and bludgeoned.

There was nothing.

Outside the office entranceway, beneath a careworn gray awning, a brick wall oozed pus from a constellation of six apertures that resembled deep sex wounds. Curd studied the anomalies carefully. He sampled the pus and rubbed it in a tiny circular motion with thumb and forefinger. Felt like snot, the way it coalesced into small, hard balls.

He went inside.

Mz. Hennington was writing something on a souped-up Admiral typewriter. She typed so fast Curd could almost see the sparks shooting from her knuckles as a flurry of cyphers darted across the VDT looming over the keys. He hung up his coat, stepped behind her, and placed a hand on the satin fabric of her shoulder. She froze.

[Whiteknuckled spectators. Skewered pianists hunched onto the bloodspattered keys in weird, evil pieces. Eyes scraped out.]

"Something's wrong," he said, playing with a lock of her hair.

She didn't turn around. She sat stiffly in her chair and replied, "What's wrong?"

"I don't know. It's bad, though. Baaad." He took her by the arms, pulled her to her feet and ran his palms, slowly, with mild calculation, across the bridge of her ass. Mz. Hennington cocked her head. Smirked. Curd kicked the chair aside and pulled up her skirt and yanked down her panties, throwing her off balance. She broke a heel. Apologizing, Curd locked her elbows behind her back with the crowbar of his forearm, pushed her down onto the desktop, cheek to cherrywood, and fucked her. Slowly, tenderly, accomplishing a fine rhythm. Then rough.

[*Atrum vir astrum procul vos tergo procerus fenestra.*]

As he neared climax, something welled up in him, something other than the proverbial rich substance. A sound. A distant cry . . . for help? Maybe. Thrusting harder and harder, he glanced around the office, looking for a source, an origin . . . And the sound evolved into another creature, from steady, meek whimper to ardent, profound *screech*. An inhuman screech. A static screech, emanating from his core, rattling the framework of his sensorium. He panicked, but not enough to call it quits. He finished the job before collapsing sharply onto his knees, pain shooting up his thighs, into his groin, and then he toppled over, head smashing into the floor as if flung there. The screech retreated, dimmed, culminated in a kind of soft monkchant. Then faded to zero.

The last thing Curd remembered was the taste of it. Putrid. Metallic, electric.

[Cryptoconchoidsiphonostomata.]

• • •

"There doesn't seem to be anything wrong with you, Mr. Curd," said the doctor.

"Curd," said Curd.

The doctor scrutinized a clipboard. "Ah yes. There you are."

• • •

The coffee tasted good. Usually it tasted like diluted oil. But he actually detected a kind of nut or stuntnut flavor, and the aftertaste was ok.

He sat by himself at a corner table and looked out the window. He brought a newspaper with him, opened it to the business section, the stock market subsection, and laid it out in front of him so that he didn't look like a bum sitting there drinking coffee without purpose or interest in the goings-on of serious men.

Outside a team of construction workers held up traffic. They seemed more interested in holding up traffic than fixing the street; if they thought a vehicle might try to glide around them too quickly or aggressively, they piledrived a canny hole in the vehicle's path, sometimes railroading it, but usually just exacerbating the already pronounced frustration and anxiety of drivers. Textbook civilization. What caught Curd's eye was a pair of outrémen across the street. He could barely see them from his position, and he had to lean over and twist his neck to get a clearer look.

He pressed his nose against the glass.

The outrémen wore standard exile-ready attire. One could have easily mistaken them for flâneurs at first glance, but careful observation revealed certain nuances and enhancements about their persons that gave them away. They stood about nine or ten feet apart, like two gunslingers itching for a draw, eyes round and loud, hands at hips with fingers spread and trembling, thigh muscles flexing beneath the crylove fabric of their trousers.

This went on for half a cup of coffee.

Then the outrémen staggered towards one another, trading words. Curd couldn't be sure if they were friendly or hostile, or even coherent, and on a few occasions the outrémen cried out and emitted haunting growls. They moved forward in a broken lurch. Petty interest threaded into raw fascination when, for a moment, Curd suspected they might merge, and kiss; their tilted faces came closer, as if on rails, ensuring no other outcome than lips on lips. He was on the verge of shouting, "They're going to kiss!"

but he caught his breath, almost choking, feeling like he had swallowed his Adam's apple.

Calmly, the outrémen feasted on one another.

It began with a simple nip, a minuscule portion of flesh that the outréman on the left removed from the cheek of the outréman on the right. A thin curve of blood spouted from the wound like water from a drinking fountain. The injured outréman paused philosophically, contemplating what had happened, perhaps, but showing no sign of pain or suffering. He returned the blow tenfold. His mouth opened to an impossible angle, like the jaws of a reptile, and he grabbed his assailant by the neck and chewed off half of his head.

Quickly the encounter escalated.

They consumed each other with increasing ferocity.

Sometimes they devoured their own bodies; as one outréman worked on his partner's intestines, for instance, his partner rolled up a sleeve and sunk prehistoric teeth into his arm like a chickenleg.

And when their teeth fell out, they used their hands, their fingernails, gouging out pound after pound of flesh, ripping off fingers and limbs.

Even when they ceased to look human, curdled on the sidewalk in a heap of quivering tissue and gristle, odd tendrils reached from the residue and lashed out, fighting to the bitter end.

Nobody noticed the gorefest. People passed by or side-stepped the outrémen as if they were dead signage.

Curd turned his attention to the café. It was empty.

Curd turned his attention to his coffee.

It was full.

• • •

It took him several minutes to get shitfaced. He ordered a beer and a bottle of absinthe and drank them as fast as he could, pausing to burp, gag, and swab his mouth with a bartowel.

Intoxication hit him like an uppercut and his shoulders dislocated. He slouched over, dizzy, deranged, a certifiable asshole, pupils dilating and contracting, pupils swallowing his eyeballs, irises, whites and all . . .

"Mooom!!!" he cried into a payphone.

"Sergio? Is that you?" said a voice.

"Moooooom!!!"

The line went dead.

He hung up the phone and hailed a smartcab, bellowing for a driver to pull over.

"You're still inside the bar," said the bartender.

• • •

Everything was normal, more or less, except on those rare occasions when people imploded, flesh folding into flesh, into a tertiary nodule, then disappearing into a vaporized bead of blood.

• • •

Curd bought a hot dog from a vending cart. No matter what happened, there were always hot dogs. He had lived on them as a child, partly because it was all his mother could afford. But he liked them. Then and now, hot dogs had always taken him away, allowed him to forget about the hardships, if only momentarily, of day after day after dayafterday . . .

• • •

Wrapped in a damp towel, Mz. Hennington slid on gold-rimmed bifocals and went to the kitchen to get something to eat. She opened the refrigerator. Stared inside. Closed the refrigerator. Opened the freezer. Stared inside. Closed the freezer.

She went back to the bedroom.

"What's with all the sausage?" she asked. "There's, like, a million hot dogs in the fridge. And beer."

Curd lay in bed fingering a revolver. "Lips and assholes."

"What?"

"Lips and assholes. Like I said."

Mz. Hennington unwrapped the towel and held her breasts in place with a forearm as she bent over and picked up her bra. "I'm going to work."

Curd rolled onto his stomach. "That's what hot dogs are made of," he mumbled into a pillow. "Lips and assholes. Residua. Detritus."

"Did you say Plotinus?"

"What?"

"Plotinus. The philosopher."

"[Pleasure and distress, fear and courage, desire and aversion—where is the seat of these affections and experiences?]"

"[Idaho?]"

Mz. Hennington fastened the bra. A deep line of cleavage sprung to life. Hurriedly she slipped on panties and hose and a lavender garter belt. "Aren't you coming?"

Still facedown in the pillow, Curd muttered something inaudible. He continued muttering as Mz. Hennington yanked up and zipped a snug business skirt into place and buttoned a cream blouse to the nape of her cleavage. "I can't hear you," she said.

Curd rolled over, arms splayed out on the bed. In one hand he gripped the revolver firmly by the barrel. "I'm not going to work today."

Mz. Hennington's smooth white calf muscles flared as she stepped into sleek high heels. "I'm going to work," she repeated.

"I'm never going to work again," said Curd. "I want to see if things will get done and if I'll still make money if I don't do anything."

Mz. Hennington sighed. "I'll just have to do everything myself. I want a raise."

"No," Curd beckoned. "I don't want you to go either. It's an experiment. Come back to bed. Let's just see what happens. Take your clothes off. Let's stay here and see what happens. Take your clothes off."

"But who will do the work? It's only us."

"Maybe the work will do itself. Get your ass over here. Please?"

• • •

"I could use a cold beer." Curd took a sip of the beer in his hand. "Ahh." He sat up in bed and leaned against the leather headboard, fingering a small red mole on his chest. As always, he wondered if it was cancerous.

Mz. Hennington tried to bite him.

He pushed her away. "Knock it off," he said. "I'm done. Maybe that's the problem. Maybe we've been having too much sex. Anything in excess is bad for you, right? Even water. And we're made of water. So is the earth. Water—and magma."

A dull groan escaped the slash of her mouth. She leaned in and snapped her mandibles together.

"Cut it out." Curd pushed her off the bed. She hit the floor hard. He turned onto his side and blinked at a portrait on the wall. It had been hanging there since he moved in. Former occupants left it behind; they nailed it to the wall with railroad spikes. Curd would have needed a crowbar to pry it off, and he had never gotten around to the job, even though he disliked the portrait. It was a Picasso. Authenticated and original, according to the label in the bottom corner of the frame. Title: "Pour Roby." It was just a rudimentary sketch, a doodle of a face that the artist no doubt produced with a few flicks of the wrist. A squiggle of hair loomed over two swollen eyes, peering innocently to the left. The nose was a long, thin, semi-distorted U, and only an upperlip defined the mouth. One ovular curve for the chin and cheeks. And beneath the face, Picasso's signature, slanted, and backwards, like a mirror image. The more Curd studied it, the more he hated it.

On the third attempt, Mz. Hennington made purchase, biting into Curd's kidney region and claiming a chunk of flesh. Stringy and elastic, it came off like latex.

Blood left the wound in steady, powerful surges.

• • •

In the dream, he's an estranged computer salesman. There are no clients.

Telephones are illegal.

He must travel from door to door, coldcalling innocent homeowners.

Most of the homeowners turn him away. The ones that let him in invariably want to buy a computer; they express this desire in highpitched, enthusiastic tones.

Just as an exchange is about to take place, however, he invariably lifts the product over his head and smashes it on the client.

The client screams and begs for mercy.

He continues to smash the client.

He becomes familiar with the sound of cracking skulls and bones. But there is no blood.

Blood is illegal.

Then he stands on the edge of a long diving board that dips halfway into the deep end.

No water in the pool.

At the blue bottom is a pile of green seaweed. It glistens with moisture in the white sunlight.

In his headspace, the quillbone of rhymed poetry . . .

• • •

The desktop was smooth and bogus and irksome. He had requested real wood, pine, but they sold him a plastic desk stained with fake wood finish. They told him it would be better this way since real wood didn't last and had to be lacquered and relacquered all the time. "Plastic lasts forever," they concluded.

He placed his ear against the desktop. It resounded like a conch shell. Tall, distant waves broke against an ivory shore.

Outside, thunder merged with turbines, exhaust pipes, the exigency of acceleration.

He focused on the radio. Light Classical. An adagio. Careful strings and soft woodwinds. He imagined a clichéd pastoral landscape: placid green savannah, tall trees with leaves rustled by the breeze, blue dome of sky—a landscape hanging on the walls of countless motels . . .

His eyelids weakened. Vague trace of a smile.

His eyes closed.

A metallic voice abruptly interrupted the music: "This program is brought to you by the Bureau of Me. Pardon the interruption. This is a test."

Rainbow of barcodes. Ringing noise.

• • •

DMV. Disgruntling Metaphysical Victimization.

Curd sat in a plastic bucket seat waiting to renew license plates for a vehicle he never used and didn't work. He wasn't even sure he owned a vehicle anymore.

It began as a harmless yawn. Even Curd was surprised when the yawn, after reaching its ostensible peak, refused to diminish, to taper off and disappear, rendering his mouth the aggrieved slit worn by all occupants of the

DMV. But the yawn grew wider, and larger, in synch with a lump in his throat that seemed to be expanding, worming its way up and out of his mouth. Furiously he tried to swallow the lump—image of an Adam's apple twitching epileptically—but nothing could be done. He felt his jaws extend. He felt his teeth rattle in his gums. Momentarily he thought his jaw might snap backwards, like a mousetrap, and consume his head, unleashing a strangled, flailing tonguebeast. Such an absurdity was impossible, though, and Curd knew it, so he turned to the man sitting next to him, an unassuming migrant worker filling out an unassuming form, and buried the yawn in his chest.

Something wet splattered onto the linoleum floor of the DMV, spit there like a cosmic pinch of tobacco.

INTERMISSION

"In Time, Reality fails. It dries up like a mushroom in the sun, and we have no choice but to machinate the Technology. There is an infinite spectrum of alternate realities. In the best realities, mankind approaches perfection, utopia, the epitome of social rest and relaxation; in the worst, mankind is devolved, zombified, fiercely aggressive and murderous—if nothing else, *estranged*. We give mankind what he wants. Like the Engines of Night, Desire makes the world turn," said a figure.

"One man in the company of Selfhood. This is a Bad Grindhouse. This is the debut of Cellular Discord. Barc-thighed schoolgirls frolic in the savannah and the Universe is a dead pig turning on the Spit," said a figure.

"And yet *he* is the Rub. The Idaho Reality threatens to consume Metaphysical Infinity. Without him, Paradise loses. With him, Paradise loses—but by a considerably lesser margin. As with everything, this is a matter of degrees and intensities. He must unilaterally embrace the [_____] within himself. He is, after all, entitled to shit on the world, despite overt plebiscitary roots. His soul putrefies in the Dumpster of Immanence. He exhales stardust and doesn't even know it," said a figure.

[This crucial and lengthy string of dialogue and exposition is garbled by a thousand insect shrieks.]

"Consuming one's flesh is an underrated act of attrition. One shouldn't consider the prospect of Certain Doom in these troubles times. Nor should one underestimate the Cluck; entire legions of meaning and innuendo reside within that beakmade commotion. The Idaho Reality awaits us like a nightmare in the closet. Yes. Man is a sublimely vast and menacing *terra incognita*. We must come to terms with this Machinery. The pistons, the cogs, the stickshifts—they point in one direction: Oblivion. Tomorrow I will find a way to construct an omelet without the use of eggs. Today, however, I must harvest momentum. Soon I will close my eyes and it will be dark," said a figure.

Last words. THEN THE BRACKETS COLLAPSED, INNERVATING THE HUMAN AQUARIUM.

Slowly the Bureau of Me glided across the sky.

ACT III

"Hello?"

"Who did you say you are?"

"It's me. Me."

"Me. That sounds familiar."

"Help me."

"I don't help people who don't help themselves."

"I'm not a person who helps himself. I'm your son."

"You don't care."

"I care."

"You won't change."

"I'll change. I'll try to change. Everybody changes. They have to. Otherwise they die."

"Goodbye."

"Don't go."
The line went dead.

• • •

"How did that make you feel?"

"Not good. Baaad."

"Go on."

"Whenever my mother left, to go grocery shopping or whatever, and I asked my father where she went, he told me she was dead. I cried like an asshole until she got home. Every time. My father assured me his intentions weren't vindictive. Rather, he wanted me to get used the idea that my mother would die. Because one day she would die." He paused. Contemplated. "I never got used to it."

• • •

Curd concluded that mankind was little more than a secretion. This was the conclusion that he always drew, no matter what happened to him. But he meant it now more than ever. Each time he drew the conclusion, however, he meant it more than the last time, and he didn't remember the first time he had drawn it. The conclusion lacked a point of origin. But there was no question that its certainty grew progressively firmer and more secure with each realization. And yet, in all likelihood, barring death, he would draw the conclusion again, soon, very soon, and at that time its certainty would be more pronounced than the last time, which is to say, this time. Hence certainty was an Old Wives'

Tale. Hence mankind was not a secretion, but something else. He knew nothing. The clockwork of his intellect, his perception, his ability to read the text of himself and the pages on which his identity had been scribbled—it was a proverbial bad joke. And he had never heard a joke that made him laugh. They all seemed too contrived.

An animal lurked past Curd. He couldn't tell what it was. A wolf? It was starving, gray mottled skin taut against outsized ribs. Blood dripped onto the street from ragged jaws, from a long dead tongue that hung down like a leash. The animal glanced up at Curd in passing, but it didn't growl, and it didn't stop.

• • •

She was taller than Curd, even after she kicked off the heels, and her legs were longer than the rest of her body. He worried about it, at first, but then realized that the height discrepancy wouldn't be a problem when she was on all fours. Dyed red hair complimented an emerald green blazer she wore over a black haltertop and leather pants. Blue eyes. Fake, offsized tits. An ass he couldn't complain about. Pencilthin neck that made her head look bigger than normal. But it was normal.

"Where are we?" she said, taking off the blazer and draping it over a foldout chair. She looked around the room. Mattress in the corner. Empty bag of potato chips beside it. Fifty or so empty bottles of beer scattered across the floor. A few of the bottles had been stacked into a clumsy pyramid.

Curd blinked. "Someplace safe."

She tried to go down on him, but he refuted her, noting the dire intimacy of blowjobs vis-à-vis the employment of the mouthpiece.

He fucked her in the ass. He paid her. She left.

Knock at the door. She had forgotten her blazer. Opening a fresh beer, he snatched the blazer and quick-stepped across the room and opened the door.

It wasn't her. It was somebody else.

It was her.

"What is this, a joke? How'd you change your clothes so fast?"

She titled her head, widened her eyes. She didn't have irises. Or lashes.

"Knock that shit off. This isn't a Superman comic. Superman is Klark Kent. Glasses and a comeover aren't enough to deceive real people."

He wasn't wearing glasses. And the red hair had been replaced by black hair cut like a motorcycle helmet. No discernible breasts. And he had on a kind of obscure fullbody uniform that might have been cop or robber, depending on context. But it was the same face. Precisely the same face . . . although it possessed a chitinous quality, Curd noticed, more like rind than skin.

"Fuck off," said Curd.

In a synthetic voice, the man replied, "I am from the Bureau of Me."

"The Bureau of Me? There's only one me. *Me*."

"You have forgotten about me. You have experienced a mnemonic cataclysm. I am coming inside."

"I'll kill you if you come in. I'll kill you if you don't." He took a swig of beer.

The bottle smashed against his face.

• • •

"Is this terminal ambiguity any more quixotic than Death itself? Death: utterly ordinary and commonplace, a daily occurrence experienced by thousands. And yet cosmically mysterious. The Unknown. It exists everywhere, among everybody, between the cracks and interstices of day-to-day life. Every ten seconds, somebody dies. Somebody just died within ten miles of you. Drive down the street and you'll pass a building in which somebody just died. Death is hungry and Death is obese and Death's gutsack is bigger than the universe. All of the universes. Reach out and It eludes you. Reach out and It embraces you. Context is the thing. Context—and desire."

• • •

"My aorta hurts."

"Can you feel your aorta?"

"When it hurts me I can." He stroked his chest with a finger as if to massage the instrument.

"Can you tell me what you do for a living please?"

His hand unfolded onto his chest and he inhaled deeply. "I used to do something. I don't do anything now. But I get paid. It was an experiment. It worked. I win. Winning is all that matters."

"Yes. Yes. Winning is good. A vital human endeavor. Do you understand that you are under arrest, sir?"

"If I say no, what happens next?"

D. Harlan Wilson

"This." Somebody boxed his ears. "Then this." Somebody hit him in the head with a hard, rubbercoated object. "Then things will get ugly."

Blood dribbled down his cheek and neck from the fresh wound on his temple, pooling in the scrapes and scabs of older wounds. He could hear the blood go. It sounded like an anaconda slithering across tarmac.

"Sir? Do you understand?"

"My answer is: *No*. My answer is: *I don't understand*."

• • •

Things got ugly. But not in the way that the arresting officer had hoped, envisioned, or planned on. Curd exploded on the cophouse with cephalopodic rage and efficiency. Bodies flapped across the room and smashed into walls and exploded through ceiling panels. Unscathed regulators drew their firearms, but they didn't know why, even when limbs started coming off and the scene turned into a holocaust.

Curd was too fast.

He eluded detection with the same effortlessness that he eluded bullets. The regulators fired into the void, trading confused and terrified glances, until there was only one man left, crazed, squealing, firing a compact submachine ruger in every direction. Methodically he moved his feet in quick circles and he moved the handgun up and down for maximum coverage. He didn't care what he hit or who he hit, as long as whatever was happening stopped happening. He went through six clips, loading and reloading in seconds, remembering his training.

43

When he ran out of ammunition, there was a long pause during which he stopped squealing and surveyed the ruins of the cophouse and tried to process the grisly spectacle. He was studying a particularly unsettling piece of debris when he suffered an intracranial hemorrhage. For an instant he was able to watch the blood spew from his eye sockets.

• • •

Now he was really lost.

Remember. Re-member. The reclamation of a lost member.

Memory.

Ember.

. . . He remembered the night he found himself in St. Louis, somehow, at three in the morning, stumbling past one wrecked and rubbled brickhouse after another. Above him the mirrorplated Gateway Arch shone, flashed, and scintillated as it reflected the neon rays beamed into space by the knot of casino-fortresses beneath it. He had been drinking tequila, a substance he abused rarely given a slight neurological allergy to blue agave plants, tequila's base ingredient. Two or three slammers rendered him a kind of disabled person; he lost the feeling in parts of his face, which slumped, and he altogether lost the ability to complete full sentences. That night he had slammed close to twenty shots of Quervo. The glut had produced the opposite effekt. Not only could he feel his face, it felt like another face had been superimposed on top, and he had Babylonian access to all of the nerve endings. Additionally, he spoke like a Julliardtrained actor; by the time he left the bar, nothing exited his mouth but crisply articulated soliloquies. He left with a girl, but she ducked into a transport hub during a particularly long and uninspiring soliloquy that plagiarized, reinvented and mocked Shakespearean rhetoric, sometimes in the same hot breath.

History wilted, died.

Alone, he grew weary.

The booze settled in, fatigue settled in.

He stumbled beneath an abandoned scaffolding frame and meandered through a maze of iron tubes and clamps. Sidestepping outrémen and squatters, he tried to remember where he was, what street he was on. No use. But he kept moving forward, and eventually he had to lean against an underdone pillar of cement to catch his breath. He considered curling onto the ground and taking a quick nap. But if he fell asleep he would stay asleep. He had to get out, to get home, or to a hotel. Somewhere . . .

He got to a phone booth. Encoded a number.

Nobody picked up. The answering machine said, "You have reached [static screech]. I am not home right now. Please [static screech]."

Dial tone.

It would have to suffice. He needed something to talk to. A dry hum was better than nothing. Metronomes of anxiety flooded his system, emanating from the tender pulse of a jugular.

"I feel real bad," he said. "Real. Bad."

He didn't know what else to say. Time passed. The dial tone purred in his ear. The city stirred in the distance, döpplering, retreating into oblivion like fog at dusk.

"I plan to stop drinking soon. I have a plan." He cocked his head, tabulating the lie. "I miss my secretary. She was very excellent at her job. Very, very excellent. I'm not just saying that . . . I've been making a concerted effort to see the good in people. And me. I'm a good person, deep down there."

He noticed his hand. The ghostwhite fingers, crooked and skeletal, with flayed cuticles, splintered nails, weird blue lines that looked more like circuit strings than desiccated veins. He moved the fingers across the shaft of the phone to make sure they still belonged to him.

He looked up. The firelights of the booth coughed and flickered.

"I don't know what's wrong with me. Something's wrong. But I can't express it. I can't say it. I wish the future didn't happen all the time. It's always happening. It's always stealing the present and changing the past."

He started to cry.

He blubbered inarticulately for a long time. Soon he forgot what he was saying, or wanted to say.

He sniffled. He caught his breath.

"I gotta . . . go . . . . . . I [static screech]."

• • •

. . . wandered into an aborted carnival, striped tents expanding across the desert from a nuclear carousel. Gold beams impaled the rotting corpses of horses.

Far overhead, static gondolas creaked weakly on loose, rusted cables.

There were no insects but thousands of frogs . . .

Drained, he rested on a bench, knees cracking like dry twigs as he sat down.

Sterterous breaths. Menacing heart palpitations.

He closed his eyes and inhaled, exhaled.

Coughed and dryheaved.

Panted.

Moaned.

Spit up impossible quantities of substances too alien to reflect on.

Afterwards he felt better. Then worse. The fibrillations of his heart produced one shockwave of anxiety and dread after another. He forced himself to stand. To walk. Motion deflecting the fear of death.

. . . wandered past a large wooden sign that said BEWARE PICKPOCKETS AND LOOSE WOMEN and found himself at the window of a foodstand.

Beat.

Beat.

Beat.

A long chalkboard menu hung over a grill of dried oil. Somebody had removed the burners. A few of the letters and numbers on the menu were smudged or wiped off, but he could still make out most of the items. Double Cheeseburger. Vinegar Fries. Cotton Candy.

Purple Cow.

Beat. Beat.

He couldn't believe it. Grape soda and vanilla ice cream. A simple drink. The greatest drink. He had never seen it for sale before, anywhere. Beat. His mother used to make Purple Cows for him. Only him. The neighborhood kids looked on in envy, pining for a hungry sip . . .

He awoke in the front car of a rollercoaster, cheek against concrete. Seatbelt on. The vehicle lay on its side, on the ground. The husk of a vast, dead centipede.

Noosphere.

Fleeting embers of memory. Revised.

• • •

"To be impaled by the erect tendrils of Life. It is not easy. It inhibits attitude control. And it always leads to the same place: INFANCY."

Dull roar of thrusters . . .

• • •

At some point his ear sealed over. The left ear. He could still hear out of it, if he concentrated. But the orifice was gone. And there was nothing to hear.

He tried not to look down. The sight of his torso, beachweathered skin sucked against spine . . . a ghastly, insufferable image. And there was a new hole. A skin ulcer. He might have been a deflating balloon. Every slow step produced a flatulent noise, emanating from the hip.

It was hot and there was no wind and no clouds.

With the sun at his back, baking the rotten skin, the landscape unfolded before him like a shadow of meaning. Architectures of flesh and foliage and technology re-treated into the cracked earth, and he conjured images of himself, old and faded images, disavowed memories, still shots of white teeth, the dawn of laughter. Hair tousled by the breeze.

THE IDAHO REALITY

A Series of Intimately Disconnected Vignettes in Which the Auteur Aspires to Formulate the Round Character (viz., the Idiot) (viz., the Blasé Subject) Who Exists in an Astonishing Narrative Diegesis That, in Union with a Skillful & Suspenseful Plot, Capable & Superior Readers Will Doubtless Perceive as the "Very Definition of Good Fiction"

The Decline of Western Civilization

This particular Decline began when she asked Seneca Beaulac if he was already dead.

"Idaho," he whispered.

Derailed, she tried her best to parry the obscene blow of negativism. Beaulac wouldn't allow it. He gestured with a thumb.

The red hallway stretched away from them and converged into a pupil of darkness.

Blotched copper.

Ding.

Elevator doors slid open. They stepped inside the mirrored chamber.

Gnarled effigies döpplered into obscurity.

She had redefined the vertiable shape of her eyes with futureshock mascara. She blinked, hard, at haphazard intervals, as if in protest of the mascara, its antagonism. She didn't wear lipstick. Beaulac studied her face, then gave her a once over, registering the dire private parts.

She fumbled with the buttons on the control panel and entered the wrong sequence. The elevator reprimanded her. With great care, she entered the correct sequence, and the elevator congratulated her, sarcastically. Beaulac watched her fingers and flexed his jaw.

Swallowing dry air, she said, "Well, at least—"

"I don't like this elevator," snapped Beaulac.

The elevator made a nervous throat-clearing sound.

Beaulac glared at the woman's reflection in the door panel and delivered a long, mostly irrational grievance on the subject of mankind. On occasion he looked directly into her eyes, at which point he made certain to maneuver his lips out of synch with his manic articulations.

The elevator stopped three times on the way up. Nobody else got on.

Ding. Roof level.

The door opened and they emerged onto a landing pad with a flourish of impetuous brass and lean percussion. Beaulac got mad. The woman moved forward.

A Byronic laugh preceded the clank of the elevator doors.

Ashclouds hung in the sky, motionless, like frayed barcodes. They walked across the rooftop to a waiting station. Beaulac ordered a coffee from a blowhole. Black. The blowhole extracted payment with a syringe, added cream and sugar, and served the coffee cold. Beaulac drank it without complaint, then crushed the cup and tossed it over his shoulder.

He punched the blowhole.

The woman tried to ignore him. She couldn't. Even though he had more or less forgotten about her.

"Can I ask you something?" she said.

An ashcloud exploded into blackfire as a subcopter fell through it and descended onto the landing pad, engine humming and whirring, blades roaring and thundering, creating a vacuum effekt that sucked her waist-length hair into a wild spiral above her head. She felt herself lifted upwards, onto her toes. Screamed. Beaulac observed her idly, trying to light a cigarette despite the maelstrom of wind. He wondered if she would float away. She was slight. He had seen people twice her size sucked into the void.

The subcopter's blades decelerated. Segments hissed open and a swell of shadows emptied onto the tarmac.

She stepped on first, conscious of Beaulac's eyes on her ass.

The subcopter waited for five minutes. Nobody else got on.

With an emphysemic blast of iron, it lifted off the rooftop like a wounded centipede, end-segments flaccid.

The lights flickered, sparks flew from bamboo filaments as they penetrated the troposphere and fell into a steady flowfugue. Beaulac sat hunched over with his mouth half open and his eyes half closed. She sat a few seats behind him, waiting for him to make a crass remark.

"What's your name?" he remarked crassly.

She chewed the makeup from her underlip.

Beaulac didn't repeat himself.

She told him her name.

"That's not a name. That's a mytzlplk." He looked over his shoulder and eyeballed her.

And they drifted towards one another as if underwater, or outer space, gravity a distant memory, an earthbound disease for which they had discovered a terminal serum. Beaulac's fingers plunged into her hair and gripped the back of her neck, squeezing the hard, warm cords.

They rolled across the compartment. Frenetic, impassioned. Limbs locked and unlocked, flesh against flesh, and fingertips strummed hungry orifices, and sanctimonious acoustics poured out of the walls with greater and greater concentration, getting stronger, angrier.

It was too dramatic. Categorically so. Even Beaulac recognized and acknowledged the Excess, and he was the star of the show. And yet the Excess continued to inflate, the drama to unfold.

A View from the Blindside

Long ago, Boise spread across the expanse of the state with bubonic angst, infecting the land, ruining its flora and fauna, and the city's grave architectures flattened the painted mountains. The city died. Only the jagged husk remained, a benign growth decaying on the scales of the earth. Overhead the immolated sky moved and undulated like a great tapestry of fireflies jockeying for position.

Idaho once had a reputation for spuds, dust, proles, and spontaneous evaporation. Props á la Steinbeck. And Oz before the tornado. But it was much more than that. It wasn't that at all.

[Description of the topography of Idaho from the sky. Segue to the man who conquered Idaho with nothing but a Fujikawan pickaxe and an absolute, if unfathomable, will to power. Invoke Nietzsche. Invoke Nietzsche in every sentence, somehow. Descended from the Balthazar dynasty, the conqueror of Idaho, who came to be known by the catchphrase "Must Obliterate All Dirned Buttes" (pronounced "Muad'Dib" in shortened, quasiacronymic form), possesses certain distinguishing features. These features also belong to the star of the soap opera based on Muad'Dib's deeds. The rub: they belonged to him long before he auditioned for the role. Like Jack Torrance, he has always been the moonraker.]

. . . Hence we encounter the palimpsest of *The Idaho Reality*, an extrapolated adaptation of the long-defunct *Ryan's Hope*, the "organic" syndication of which had been anachronistically retrofitted and dubbed according to contemporary vogue and desire. The setting of the original image-text had been New York City. As a first order of business, writers superimposed NYC with the entirety of post-Boise, Idaho, before post-Boise actually existed. At this point, the "mise-en-scène" was sheer science fiction, and there were few indications that the science fictionalization of reality (i.e., the realization of outréality) would occur. But one can't jumpstart an electrochemical cell without an etc., etc., etc.

Screen upon screen upon screen.

Socius upon diegesis upon fuckscene.

Veracity upon the Blue Loch.

Beneath the cold, clear waters, miles deep, fathoms down, a sleeper awaits the Awakening. Consciousness will produce the Fully Developed Soldier of the Mundane, the Tedious, the Exotically Ordinary and Formulaic. The stuff of history. The stuff that has appeared in limitless tomes of kingly representation.

Memory of the Shed

A large, dark shed along the desolate tract. Mnemonic thunder. The radium dial paintings . . .

On stage, an old glamrocker—tight black tapered jeans, gutflab, blousy black shirt unbuttoned to the unshorn navel, deep orange tan, sagging neckskin, bleached jaws, matted curly hair like a dead hedgeplant—leaped out from behind a banister, hit a high note (*tenore contraltino*, the highest possible male register), and took refuge behind the banister again, denying his one-man audience too long of a glimpse. Woofers thumped. Piezoelectric guitars blasted from loudspeakers.

A discoball spat diluted squares of light onto the corroded hardwood floor.

Moravagine.

Whenever the client's glass went dry, a stickthin waiter stepped out of a shadow and refilled it with the finest pinot noir in the shed. The client gave him a dirty look every time, then tested and studied the legs of the wine for at least half a minute, rocking the bulb of the glass in his palm. He always spit out the first sip, on the floor, the table sometimes, and bellowed in disgust. Then he drank half the glass and nursed the rest.

The client drank until he got drunk. And he drank more, and more, scenes from monochromatic action blockbusters running across the mindscreen at increased speeds as he struggled to abort dreams of profound heartache juxtaposed with undue expressions of affection.

The Idaho Reality

The main character of the soap opera wore the same outfit in every episode: flipflops, corduroy slackpants, roomy longsleeved wheatgrown white shirt. This was not an acceptable ensemble, and it certainly wasn't the ensemble itemized in his contract. In the early days of the role, he conceded to the terms of the contract, at least in the case of bodygear and its vicissitudes. Somewhere between the fiftieth and sixtieth episode, however, he grew weary of costume changes, and he came to the listless conclusion that he would wear what he wanted, something comfortable, something airy and formlessly fitted, and everybody else—the director, the grips, the naysayers in between—would let him do what he wanted, since he was the star

D. Harlan Wilson

of the show and ratings would suffer beyond repair even in the days or weeks it would take to replace him with another, equally (in)capable actor, who would require the audience to suspend their disbelief, as a new, different actor would suddenly be in the position of the old, obstinate actor, who might actually find that life wasn't so bad, sipping lizardgreen margaritas on the lush peak of a fell overlooking a cool blue tarn in his Own Private Idaho.

Incidentally, on the issue of suspension of disbelief, the audience had already been required to do so vis-à-vis the protagonist's attire. In fact, at the beginning of every show, and whenever a costume change was supposed to occur, subtitles warned viewers to pretend that he wore this or that garment, despite what he actually wore, as this or that garment reflected the psychological economy of his character, whereas the flipflops, the slackpants, etc. merely reflected the actor's authentic desire, or lack thereof. In addition to the subtitles, the actor, for the sake of human idiocy, as a kind of insignia of that idiocy, agreed to wear a sign on his chest that reified the subtitles, e.g., at the beginning of episode ninety-six, he pranced on-scene wearing flipflops, slackpants, etc. and a sign that read

ADDIDAS SNEAKERS
ACIDWASHED JEANS
ETC.

and in the third act of episode three thousand and one a sign that read

GLINTING CORDOVAN PENNYLOAFERS

CUFFLESS PINSTRIPE NAVYBLUE SLACKS
ETC.

and once he wore a sign that read

CECI N'EST PAS UNE PIPE

only instead of accompanying the image of a pipe, the text hung beneath a photograph of an inconspicuous bald man with pinprick eyes and poorly applied pince-nez. A joke on his part. But such monkeybusiness was rare, and generally the actor and protagonist and star (viz., *Curd*) bore the signs in good humor, ensuring that the audience was not bamboozled to the point of no return. Hence he accomplished a fertile mediation between reality and fantasy, according to some critics. Others elected to turn a blind eye on the foremost specter of *The Idaho Reality*.

Curd's penchant for assholery of this nature under-went a slow cultivation. On and off the set. Moneymen, authoritarians, colleagues and underlings loved him and hated him. Fans generally loved him, unless they met him in person, in which case they came to despise him like unleashed, unwanted kernels of repression, wishing they could bury the kernels again, until they returned *à l'écran* to *The Idaho Reality*, and their obsession with the cult of celebrity dissolved the Odium. Curd had a way of wiping mnemonic slates clean. Something in the prowess, the dynamism of his performances, which, objectively con-ceived, were quite poor, almost silly, unintentionally, as if he had no acting experience or training whatsoever, and if he did, as if he aspired to subvert that experience and training at every turn, remorseful, sometimes appalled, that he had ever acquired it.

And yet.

In virtually every shot, Curd interacted against the Vile Canvas. Silent movies summoned from covert projectors and pixels threatened to overthrow the prevailing diegesis. Marginalized lifescapes didn't stand a chance.

. . . and Curd crashed *The Red Sky at Night Show*. He had not been slated as a guest, but he showed up anyway, knocking out the keynote celebrity in his dressing room with a Tiffany lamp. He sashayed onto the set to a tuneful (but suddenly mystified) gust of brass, doing a semi-coordinated jig, and then he groaned into the corner of a long leather chair, legs splayed, wearing a tumble-dried leisure suit from which he removed and shotgunned a tall silver Asahi. He belched. He crushed the empty can and kicked a cup of coffee off of the table in front of him. Ready for anything, the host, Conrad Oakperson, deflected the intrusion with indisputable normalcy and a handful of out-of-the-corner-of-the-mouthisms. They talked, exchanging compliments and willful diatribes. Things went well. Curd assured Oakperson that *The Idaho Reality* was a "great place to work," a "real fulfilling experience," run by folks who were at "the top of their game." Then, unexpectedly, he got mad. Nothing in particular set him off. He and Oakperson were exploring the issue of anti-aging skin creams. And Curd said, "Yeah, that's true. That's very true. Well. F@#$. I don't know. Really I don't. But the problem with everybody is they're a bunch of f@#$heads. I mean, %@$&^#*$*&$#($%!!! Everybody wants to be me. And I want to be everybody else. F@#$ everybody. And f@#$ me." The imprint from the verbal suckerpunch seemed to linger on Oakperson's smooth bronze cheek. Curd was drunk, per usual, but on wine, not scotch or vodka, so it could have been much worse, and he didn't get in a fight with anybody in the audience or even backstage after the show, barring a short scrap with the keynote celebrity, who had returned to consciousness and ambushed him, but another Tiffany lamp put an end to further aggression. And later that night, after he had gotten in a fight with a call girl and trashed a hotel room, he told the cops that a wild armadillo had finagled its way through an open window (on the 36th floor) and tore everything to shit. "The animal was the culprit," he assured a de facto newscrew. He lingered on a busy streetcorner in a bright white bathrobe. "That broad and me, we could only do our best to evade the beast and try to kill it," he informed a cluster of pulsing microphones behind which flashbulbs exploded like supernovas. "We used the furniture. Chairs. Ottomans. Stuff like that. Who doesn't want to kill an intruder? I even dislodged a mirror from the bathroom and smashed it on the f@#$er, but it was too quick, or too strong. It was an armadillo. Do you know how mean armadillos are? They're mean."

Days passed and everything was recorded, replayed, fetishized. Forgotten.

"It's not that easy playing the same dumb character over and over again. Ask anybody." Curd looked around the studio. Set against a row of clumsy partitions, the gaunt faces shattered the rules of banal magnetism. Curd dryheaved and said, "It's not about stamina. Leave that to the s&%!eaters. I'm talking about soul murder. I'm a victim. Hack me open and you'll see nothing but stardust, hear nothing but a dry whistle. The character becomes more real than the real you. And the real you is a fiction. A multiple fiction. An infinite fiction. I'm not complaining. I'm only saying f@#$ everybody. And f@#$ me. I just want to be left alone."

Feelings of inadequacy. The body as prosthesis. Consciousness as epiphenomenon.

In spite of certain misanthropy, however, Curd flew into a rage whenever he went unnoticed in public for more than a reasonable duration, accusing guilty parties of ignoring him simply to prove a point. "If we're forced to live among one another," he rationalized, "we might at least exercise the bareknuckled social niceties."

A Snarl of Wind

accompanies a tracking shot all the way from sunny Coeur
D'Alene . . . . . . to thunderstruck Montpelier. The theme
song ends abruptly, with a choking of aerophones.

The Good Director

He—and it is always-already a *he*, phallic insecurities necessitating cosmic elements of control—tells the actors when scenes will be shot in slow motion. Despite the gravest talent, nobody can act truly natural with the knowledge of being unnaturally inscribed onto "celluloid." Following a brief period of compensatory overconfidence during which the actors move their arms and lips with animation, they proceed to exhibit vague traces of inhuman minutia, attempting to act normal, to negotiate the fabric of realtime, but of course this fabric—the knowledge of its illusory form with respect to the ensuing Screen—discombobulates them, as they know, mindfully, in those esoteric moments, that they are being subject to slowtime, if only by the camera, while "existing," so to speak, as both actors and people, in realtime. The good director plants this seed. Then he shoots the scene in realtime and unleashes it on the world, *au naturel*, like a dragoon of sledgehammers hurled at the cheapseats with wild precision.

Yellow Mike

. . . and remembered summer camp. Like all the bourgeois subjects. Bugjuice in the cafeteria. Quiet wetdreams in the sleeping bag. Ghost stories around the firepit.

It was at Camp Manitou-Lin. Northern Michigan. The smell of dank log cabins returned to Curd at least once a day, unsuspectingly, insidiously. He breathed in the content and struggled to process it.

[THE LEGEND OF YELLOW MIKE (mnemonic remix). The creature/man is either a nascent sasquatch or a (d)evolved human. Distinguished by mustard yellow fur/hair. Lived in a city, somewhere in West Virginia, post-autogeddon, smokestacks set against the dead, bald mountains. He had been stabbed in the eye with a syringe.

Long story. And the eye grew back with mystic, Gorgonic vehemence, capable of hypnotizing victims momentarily, just long enough for Yellow Mike to maul and on occasion disembowel them with freakish claws/fingernails. No motive other than assholery with a touch of bitterness apropos the proverbial traumatic kernel.]

Curd's thoughts turned to a crib. It might have been his, once. But he was older now.

Mahogany bars. Skyblue sheets.

Somebody was in there, folded into a corner, imploded, like a crushed oilcan.

Somebody. Something.

Fibrous, glistening wings folded around the core frame. And a design on the wings, a mirror image, green and sharp and magnetic. The arms were human, sinewy, wrapped around pointed knees. There was no face. Two red eyes loomed over a sad, sallow grin.

Where did the baby go? Had there ever been a baby?

Curd stood in the doorway and watched the creature breathe. Terror numbed the senses. He froze in these situations. It wasn't like being behind the camera. Reality, consciously perceived and experienced, was a very different animal.

A camp counselor approached the climax of an episode of *Yellow Mike*.

Curd passed out, unable to process the horror from the standpoint of consciousness. Unconsciously, however, everything operated according to the "rules." The dogs of clarity effervesced and sprinted across his field of vision. He knew what he was. He knew what the cosmos was. He knew he could kill Yellow Mike, but chose not to. He knew that futurity was contingent upon his desire, his will. The grasshopper's long-legged song.

Magnetic Attraction Enhancing Bodywash

She spoke through an esophagul exodus of chili. "God just wasn't ready to put me in my cage yet. (Swallow.) I was dead, more or less. *Dead*. (Swallow.) But they fixed me. I don't know how they did it. I owe those men my life. (Swallow.) My *life*. I can't wait to get into my cage but it's not gonna happen because of this old spleen now. (Swallow.) I don't like this fuckin' chili. (Swallow.) Where's the waiter? Waiter. Waiter." A meek interlocutor sat across the table, nibbling French fries and agreeing with the woman who might have been her daughter, or her granddaughter, or possibly a sister. Difficult to say from this perspective.

"There aren't any waiters here."

She swallowed the last spoonful of chili and licked the rim of the cardboard bowl clean. "I'm only saying, is all. When I order something to eat I expect it to taste good. That didn't taste good and somebody should do something about it. But I'm alive. Do you know what that means? It means that . . ."

As she continued, a grinning man with silver hair slipped in front of the table, coattails masking the women's faces. "I am the Coda," he intoned, and lifted his arm. He held a large green bottle. The label read:

MAGNETIC ATTRACTION ENHANCING BODYWASH

The bottle grew larger and larger, engulfing the scene, and the label began to glow. Then:

Savannah and wind. And sky. Clouds moved across the rosewood vastness like the phantoms of slugs.

And finally, gently, we return to *The Idaho Reality*.

The Fall of Greased Lightning

Seneca Beaulac raced down the street with a 600 lb. refrigerator full of sand strapped to his back. Seconds ago,
he knocked out a stuntman (i.e., a stuntman playing a
stuntman) who had been garishly stretching his legs and
cracking his neck in preparation for the feat. But Beaulac
was stubborn, driven. Likewise the actor beneath the
Satin Sheets . . .

Nobody expected it.

Nobody knew what to do.

Everybody tried to stay in character.

Cameramen shot authentic footage of cameramen
shooting faux footage of a wide-eyed director, Roy Poole,
who fucked up his lines and shouted out garbled orders

from a highchair. Perched atop a great knoll of tracking equipment, the real director, Johnson Bakos, reprimanded Poole with a *bouche forte*-chic red megaphone, but Bakos told the crew to keep shooting; they'd seen worse, much worse, and they'd make this scene work yet.

Caught off guard, Jack Fenelli, Beaulac's opponent, here and in matters of the heart, balked at the starting line; he fell forward like a strongman's mallet. And he had been slated to win the race in the script. The backside of the refrigerator strapped to his back had been decorated with a flashy turbothruster. Beneath the image, this sobriquet:

GREASED LIGHTNING

The refrigerator crushed Fenelli and he sort of exploded, veins and vines of gore skittering across the pavement, blood spattering the horrified and underpaid extras that surrounded the improv spectacle, wondering whether they should cheer or run away. They looked to Bakos for guidance. Bakos made an imperiled frogface.

Stencilists had not yet doctored Beaulac's refrigerator.

He made it to the finish line, fifty yards down Scrimm Street. He was on all fours by the time he got there, and a considerable quantity of sand had leaked from a turncoat aperture in the refrigerator door. But he made it.

Malingerers observed Beaulac in confused agitation as he rose to his feet and dispatched the refrigerator with a great bellow, then moved his arms in circles, smoothing the kinks from his rotator cuffs. At the starting line, make-shift orderlies uneasily reanimated the flattened corpse of Jack Fenelli.

Standing at her post, Sasha Crack ran her eyes up and down a palmscreen, controlling the text with a retinal line of flight. Bakos had constructed a set of Poppy Lincoln's character traits for her to memorize and internalize. Negative traits far outweighed positive ones. In fact the latter consisted of only three items:

skinny
big tits
"street smarts" (simulated)

The former, on the other hand, looked like this:

heavy smoker
anti-psychotic prescription (weaning)
pothead
clonazepam addict
terrific mood swings
emotionally volatile
vaguely bipolar
history of cancer in family
hair falling out
hairy pussy
dry cunt
issues w/body image (anorexia and/or bulimia)
obsessed w/self-portraits
promiscuous (STDs?)
allows strange men to masturbate in front of her
does not exercise
kisses/fucks like fish
white trash

lives w/parents
epileptic

Crack had read and reread and processed and reprocessed and inscribed and reinscribed the traits hundreds of times, and yet she still couldn't believe it. How broken and fucked up could this weird broad be? Typical Bakosian femme-doll, though.

Lost in a convoluted reverie that oscillated between enmity for the director and would-be empathy for the character, Crack didn't hear the clapboard. By the time she came back to herself, he was literally breathing down her neck.

She crushed the palmscreen in a fist and snapped into the mind/body apparatus of Poppy Lincoln, whirring like a dimestore stereo.

Beaulac wore a sign around his neck that read:

FUTURISTIC HIGHTOPS
TIGHT RACING PANTS
KEVLAR SLEEVELESS COLLARLESS SHIRT

In reality, he wore flipflops, corduroy slackpants, roomy longsleeved wheatgrown white shirt.

Startled, Lincoln said:

[Deadairdeadairdeadairdeadair.]

Crack couldn't remember her line.

"Line!" It happened to be the right line.

"Bitch," griped Roy Poole. He stood in front of Bakos' star cameraman, striking the same authoritative pose as his boss.

Beaulac took Lincoln by the arms and squeezed her elbows. Hard. "I'm not gonna hurt you," he said, gazing purposefully into her eyes. "I'm not gonna hurt you. I'm not gonna hurt you. I'm not gonna hurt you."

The pain was unbearable. A corrosive moan exited Lincoln's gash, lips opening onto her face like the lobes of a Venus flytrap.

"I will possess you," whispered Beaulac. Biotin-clad fingernails sunk into her flesh. "I already possess you, my love. Winners take all . . ."

A rivalry had formed three episodes ago between Roy Poole and Seneca Beaulac for the affections of Poppy Lincoln, who had slept with both characters and told both of them that she loved them unconditionally, to the "End of Time." Insane with jealousy, the faux director dashed forward—he was an older man, early sixties, but he could run all right and even gained speed, despite bowlegs and two halfass knee replacements in the left leg—with the intention of . . . he forgot what his character was supposed to do. Something violent. And he remembered that, whatever he was supposed to do, Beaulac would triumph. Quickly, cleanly, painfully. But what sort of blow or maneuver had he been scripted to execute, if only in a preliminary stage? Nothing came to him. Unlike Sasha Crack, the actor playing Poole, Neil MacCurtain, only skimmed scripts, preferring spontaneity to constructedness (or, as some detractors argued, to quality). He wasn't a good actor, but nobody was, no matter how much they prepared or practiced, or didn't. Nobody was really very good at anything in the industry. Talent had died with the modernists. Things got done, though, and dipshits got paid. Nothing else mattered.

Splitseconds before impact, MacCurtain decided that Poole would simply punch the fucker as hard as he could in the nose. He cocked his elbow.

And Seneca Beaulac, cradling Poppy Lincoln like a blunderbuss, roundhoused him on the chin, cracking and dislocating the mandible. Poole went down like an anvil. He struck the floor face first, shattering the mandible. He tried to scream but could only gurgle and choke as gore flowed out of his mouth and fanned across the concrete.

"Ding dong that cunt is dead," announced Bakos. Then, gesticulating at Beaulac: "Enter her now."

Martially enraged, as if a neural circuit had blown, Curd broke out of character for the first time in years, eyeballing the director. "Enter her? What kind of a thing is that to say? ENTER YOU!!!" Curd's face cracked like a broken thermometer. "You don't tell me who to fuck, primate. I fuck whoever and whatever I fucking want, whenever I fucking want, you fuckin' whore!" Normally Curd would have blitzed Bakos, but he knew the director was baiting him—poorly, of course—and he wasn't about to let Poppy Lincoln off the hook. He dipped her like a ballroom dancer, formally and with crazed exactness, and somehow he managed to work a thumb into her snatch (unscripted). She gasped. Moaned. Poole's crew moved in closer, choreographing furious beavercams, while Bakos' crew encircled the standoff and shot footage in BASIK (Bullettime Anamorphic Schizflowed Ionized Ka). Beaulac removed his thumb, flicked moisture from the nail, and pulled Lincoln erect. He ran a hand up her leg (tearing pantyhose) and waist (tearing garter belts) and across her breasts (squeezing, pinching) and finally gripped her neck like the handle of a medieval sword.

The kiss was deep.

The kiss was violent and confused and foul; drool mixed with drool and produced more drool. From certain angles, they looked like they might be trying to eat each other's heads. And yet an unquestionable erotic quality distinguished the ersatz fuckscene. Nobody could explain it—lexicons had been shrinking at an alarming rate in recent years, prompting the few vocabularians who still had manageable supplies of word hordes at their disposal to wonder if lexicons, collectively, had always-already run on empty—but they couldn't deny it either. This was the very definition of Curiosa, of Dirty Love. And Beaulac knew it. And Curd knew it. Emblazoned by a corona of epistemological certainty, he proceeded to wow onlookers, forcing them in and out of character by sheer masculine (viz., hairdo) prowess and execution and dynamism, and Poppy Lincoln, helpless, devolved into Sasha Crack, devolved into jelly, numb and stupid with ecstasy, on the cusp of reality, of sanity. She could only do her best to endure the melodrama of her lover's incontrovertible technology without submitting to the warm ogre of unconsciousness.

She failed.

Somewhere in the future, the clapboard clapped, and the credits rolled.

Memento Mori

"Sir," uttered the concierge, panicking, "there's a problem with your blood."

"Problem?" Curd licked the wound and rolled a tonguetip across the crown of his teeth, eyes on the ceiling.

The concierge shook his head in grave regret. "The appliance isn't recognizing your DNA. I am very sorry, Mr. Curd."

"*Curd*. You know my name, asshole. Run it again, asshole. What's the matter with you?" He pressed his fingers into the illuminated countertop.

"Regrettably, I've already run it three times, and the appliance only permits one trinity per draw."

"Fuck the appliance."

"Yes, sir. Perhaps another sample? One never knows."
A dim smile interrupted the concierge's aggrieved facade.

Irreality TV Show

It was to nobody in particular that he often made the off-the-cuff remark.

CURD
(deadpan)
My only real objective in life is to
tell the truth.

Then, invariably, he turned away, beveled.

The clockwork of his selfhood failed to compute the daily grind of technocultural interpellation. This happened more and more. Only one way to negotiate it: madness, fury, and hatred unleashed in no particular direction.

Homicidal gongs banged in the mnemonic distance. Soiled backpackers strummed ruined guitars in the rain, just beyond the Tall Window, on the brown grass, beside the exploded RV. The stench of loss. Love that never was and always will be.

A car door hushed shut. The sound byte produced a moment of canned euphoria.

As his portrayal of Seneca Beaulac failed to garner sufficient ratings—a common occurrence whenever the plague of an economic recession forced viewers to demolish their wallscreens with airhammers, ensuring themselves that, when the recession passed, they would be wiser for it, and they wouldn't waste their blood on another wallscreen, an act of mental strength that lasted roughly three to four days, post-recession—Curd turned to the specter of ITV (Irreality Television). IBS (Irritable Broadcasting System) agents hounded him on a regular basis, fidgeting/loitering on sets and in dressing rooms, and it was a simple matter of making eye contact. He had his own show by lunch. Ironically, all shows, ITV or non-ITV, were ITV shows; irreality informed the diegeses of every media representation in the wake of The Fjord War, a twenty-year global struggle for the "colonization" of certain Canadian glaciers believed to "hyperventilate" mysterious Pleistocene chemicals that "superevolved" the human body and mind in controlled climates. But something happened, something bad, and the glaciers died, or revolted, or evaporated, or something. Whatever the case, the catastrophe "penalized" the real world, mutated the metaphysical socioscape, reducing all cultural extensions of that socioscape to an nth degree of meaning. Either subjectivity had schized, or objective reality had schized, or both. Probably both. It didn't matter. Things didn't add up like they used to for past generations. Understandably Curd found it troubling that ITV called attention to itself as a uniquely muscled arm of capitalizm, one that wielded a monopoly on the industry, when in fact it was all the same shit, everywhere, on every channel, on every screen, the same uncanny, troubled relationship between cause and effekt, desire and the socius. Curd was sure to let the producers, writers, editors, and directors of the show know how he felt about the discrepancy before signing a contract. His intent was not to enlighten minds, make a statement, or assert identity, but rather to lessen the load of *ennui* that beleaguered his character(s) and induced massive depressions whenever he failed to lash out at the world and the shitforbrained donkeydicks that populated and ran it.

A squadron of writers mulled over the first line of the show for weeks. What should it be? How might it dynamically capture the attention of viewers while at the same time appearing off-the-cuff, pedestrian, and in some respects altogether bland and irrelevant—the key to any good preliminary hook? This is what they decided on:

CURD
(deadpan)
There are a mass of schematisms, a host of innate governing principles, that guide our social and intellectual and individual behavior.

Curd stood in a bathroom, naked, shoulders slumped forward, upside-down triangle of fuzz on the chest, clenching the shaft of a dirty toothbrush as he spoke to the camera behind the mirror. Viewers immediately identified the monologue as plagiarism. At the same time, they couldn't identify a derivative source. More problematic was that the monologue failed to accomplish its intended goal. The show was cancelled before the first episode had been shot in its entirety. And yet the first episode ran in its entirety, with beginning and middle and end, weeks later. And criticism of the show was slow to unfold. This spatiotemporal horseshit produced hallucinogenic fistfights among viewers and industry-goers alike. Curd escaped the fracas with meager flesh wounds and massive ego wuxia.

Within a year's time, possibly a month's time, no longer than half a week, or a day—Curd received word that he had won the Pulitzer.

It was the first time the award had been given to an ITV performance in lieu of exemplary investigative jour-nalism or noble media representations of Amerikan life, although the performance arguably fell into the latter category. The judges were inflexible. They hated Curd. Everybody hated Curd. But nobody could deny the artistry of his acting prowess, i.e., his ability to manifest (ir)real subjectivity, i.e., the way in which he conducted/constructed himself as an important and historic figment of reality.

He pretended to be surprised when he heard the news via idiotbox, despite pathological overconfidence in his ability to win the Pulitzer for something, at some point, in some strange matrix of implosion. He thanked Management and told them he wouldn't be able to attend the awards ceremony, whenever it was, in light of a previous engagement involving "insert bullshit here."

Origins, viz., Get Me Somebody Who Has Killed Somebody

In Which the Director Insists He Speak to a Man Who Has Killed Another Man, or a Woman, or Whoever, for Whatever Reason, by Accident, on Purpose, Etc., So That He Might Probe & More Effektively Understand (If Not Empathize with) the Posttraumatic Anxiety That Plagues the Killer, & Ultimately So That He Might Discuss & Convey This Anxiety to His Protagonist, Curd, Who Must Kill Somebody in the Next Episode, then Kill Himself & Return from the Dead, & Yet "It Must Be Understood," the Director Announces Before the Day's Introductory & Final Shoots, "This Is Not a Zombie Narrative. If Anything, It Is a Narrative About Being & Nothingness, Fear & Trembling, Exile & the Kingdom, Capitalizm & Schizophrenia . . ."

And after Curd rose from the dead, he ran through his lines with more frontal efficacy than he had perhaps ever managed to accomplish in the past.

Inevitably his thoughts turned to history. A hauntology of meaning and resonance struck him like the exclamation point of a teenage hardon. Stillshots, camcorder footage, blockbuster action sequences passed across the egoscreen.

His parents.

They manifested in a Zapruder altverse on a planet that was more earthlike than earth itself. Corroded pinks leaned into aggravated greens. Dad wore the black hat and the black suit and the thin black tie with the black shiny belt and the winedark shoes. Mom wore the retrohousewife thing. They stood in the yard and looked at Curd, faces blurring/burning in and out of focus. Synthetic remixes of Beach Boys harmonies and Alka-Seltzer jingles reified their Dire Presence.

How they didn't understand him. His artistry. From the beginnings of consciousness, he had perceived himself as a harbinger of true creative exploration, even though it would be years before he could articulate it. His parents were oblivious, then and now.

Comprehension escaped them like abused housepets.

Their awe of the simple things, the trivial things. Their condemnation of his lifestyle, even as a child.

Fort Mackinac, whitewashed and snaking, stately palisade, rested on the south face of the ripe Michigan island. Erected in the 18th century, it was the site of two seminal battles in the War of 1812 and served as a military outpost until 1985, when the gates closed. Today it served as a museum. Curd visited once a year, every summer, for a week, with the Boy Scouts (Troop 290), who patrolled the fort, standing at various posts, e.g., the gun platforms, making certain tourists didn't wander "onstage" during canon demonstrations, but generally standing there and looking hazily authoritative, and obtuse, naïve in any case, wearing kneehigh socks, skintight cargo shorts, merit badge sash across the chest, ponytail scarf strangling the neck, and on the head, a weird hat. He and his cronies got it in their minds to steal some goddamn muskets. No particular reason other than Young Male Sociopathy, and they planned it, and they did it, only, as they marched across the parade ground of the fort in broad daylight, cucumbercool, with a seasoned actor's shiteating confidence, guns slung over their shoulders in handsome burlap sacks, Jeremiah Worst tripped and impaled himself on an errant bayonet. The blade sunk into his chin at an angle and slid through the junkyard of his skull, severing the retinal cords of an eyeball, which promptly exploded from the socket and skittered across the grass, wowing spectators, terrifying them like an epileptic nightmare, and Jeremiah fell to his knees, the blade of the bayonet an antennae poking out of his weird hat, and then he fell onto his stomach, flat, in slow motion (from this point on, violence perpetually, unrelentingly unfolded in slow motion), confused, deranged . . .

Dead.

The butt of the bayonet struck a rock, forcing it to twist, to open a zipper in Jeremiah's face and empty out the Knowledge. Exodus of daytrippers. Curd ogled the spectacle of impossibly horrific Drama, mesmerized. Unlike his fellow apparatchiks, he made no effort to get away. It didn't matter. They were all apprehended and sent home in a crate.

Accordingly, Curd's parents stood in the yard and looked at him, faces blurring/burning in and out of focus.

But it was too late. It had always been too late. Curd had found his calling. Or rather, his calling had found him. Nobody could do anything about it. The dye had been shat.

Next paragraph.

Retreat to infancy. Images: orange carpet, gray walls, bunk beds with red sheets beyond the white crib, a green piñata hanging from a thin chain, and on a blue shelf, Raggedy Anne and Andy dolls arranged in polite sitting positions. At night, the dolls' faces seemed to change, somehow. To contort. Cave in. Difficult to tell if it was for better or for worse.

Technicolor mise-en-scène interrupted by orgasmic bowel movements, loving embraces, harmless vomiting, and feelings of checkered security.

Next paragraph.

Retreat to the womb . . .

We conclude with a monochrome snapshot of a marvelous cocoon, dark and webbed and nestled between the mossy roots of a vast Ugandan rainforest tree.

Mothman Sighting

[Evening. A family—Dad, Stepmother, Brats—drives down the interstate crammed into the front seat of a luxury vehicle. Christian Rock on the radio. Dad wants Country. He fumbles with the touchscreen on the dash with cumbersome fingers, momentarily taking his eyes from the road.

Stepmother: "Look out shitforbrains!"

7-8 feet tall, reflective red eyes, jack-o-lantern grin, brittle limbs with joints that swing both ways, freshly molted wings, electricity dancing in the hollow places, etc.—it crawls out of a ditch and staggers across the dark, flickering highway.

Stepmother: "Watch out shitbirrrrrd!"

Brats kick each other and kick their toys and their technologies and kick the back of the seat and the back of Dad's headrest.

Dad: "Knock it off you little shits! I'll fuckin' kill you shitbreathers!" He reaches over his shoulder and swings around his big hand like a flyswatter, hoping to hit a mark.

The luxury vehicle swerves, but not enough.

They collide with the mothman squarely, shattering its legs, and the thing endures the usual effekts: roll across hood, smash into windshield, tumble into sky, head smashes into aluminum roof, neck cracks, aluminum roof dents, wings swell and spread and flap uncontrollably from deep folds in shoulderblades, more somersaults, finally mothman is projected off of car's tailfin. Everybody screams in harmonic unison. Dad stomps on the breaks with both feet in mid-swerve and the car flips up and over like a poker chip and it tumbles down the interstate for awhile before coming to rest and exploding into impossible white flames. Like all living creatures, Dad, Stepmother and Brats die alone, skin melting onto heavy-duty, fire-resistant floormats, organs pouring from residual mouths of gore.

The mothman curls up in a ditch on the other side of the road and prepares to hibernate.]

Wreckage

When Curd was two years old (i.e., when Curd wasn't
Curd) he broke his leg. He didn't fall out of a tree, off
of a roof or ladder, or anything that has the ability to
test gravity's stranglehold on solid objects. He simply
tripped over an exposed root in the grass and took an
awkward tumble. His father had been playing with him
and witnessed the wreckage. He couldn't believe it. The
fall belonged in a cartoon. Legs weren't meant to do that,
to twist like that. And two-year-olds weren't supposed to
break bones. They were supposed to be resilient. When
he was two years old his dad bounced him around like a
basketball, tossed him around like a football, kicked him
around like a soccerball, and his bones were fine.

It was the femur. Not a compound fracture, but bad. Cracked all the way through. Doctors had to put Curd in a twenty lb. cast that wrapped around his waist and covered both of his legs. He had to sit on his ass for four weeks and not move. He had to have his diapers changed every two hours, day and night, through a small hole in the ass of the cast—an almost impossible feat that required at least two people to accomplish. He thought he was being punished. He cried and cried. Nobody could help him; cognitively he had not reached a point where he could process logic. He was two.

Shortly after the removal of the cast, he began to see things fall out of the sky and crash into the earth.

The first thing that fell was a whale.

The second thing was an elephant.

The third thing was a brontosaurus.

The fourth thing was a . . .

The animals never fell near enough so as to endanger Curd, but he could see them clearly, even if he didn't know what they were. They exploded with comic ferocity when they struck the ground and produced terrific earthquakes. As far as Curd could tell—next to nothing—adults seemed to disavow the wreckages, taking notice of them, but idly, and then forgetting about them within minutes. If, say, a hail of giant squid exploded onto the neighbor's house, destroying it, the neighbors became violently annoyed, but within seconds they had returned to the business of life, stepping over and around the residual carnage as if it had been part of the house's architecture from the beginning.

"*Du commencement*," said Curd's piano teacher, Mz. Gerdes—flashbulb of a gleaming perm—years later, as he sat in front of the keys, legs dangling from a vinyl spinning stool, and stared out the window at some creature from some children's fantasy novel he had read, racing to the earth like a flaming meteor.

Official Sobriquet vis-à-vis the Media

"Weird Menace."

In execution: "Once again, Curd a.k.a. the 'Weird Menace' established himself as a shining example of unbridled assholery, tomfoolery and pathology, singling out and knocking over old people on the red carpet last night just minutes before the opening act of the Daytime Emmy Awards. Among his victims was veteran actor John Aniston, 145, who has played the role of patriarchal mobster and monster Victor Kiriakis on *Days of Our Lives* for the past 60 years. John had this to say: 'He came out of nowhere, really, throwing elbows and so forth. In my case, he hammered on my knee with a cane until I went down. No doubt he stole the cane from somebody who needed it. It's true what they say, you know. That bastard is a weird menace.'"

Homme de mite

The long version of this vignette was lost in a stage reen-
actment of the accidental fire that burned down the library
of Alexandria. In the distant future, fossilized scraps of
the narrative were accidentally discovered by spacemen
on a routine check of the shriveled Earth. The following
document was culled and spliced together from those
very scraps:

In the interim, Curd spotted a mothman in France. In
Eze. Always in Eze, although I barely remember it, it's
been so long—ancient iron bridge hanging over the gray
tavern that slopes into the Mediterranean—quaint architectures carved into the mountainside, colorful flames of
vegetation, and down the road, Monte Carlo . . .

It was at the roulette table.

He was young and didn't know the rules. He tried to hand cash to the dealer instead of laying it on the felt like a Rolex.

Reprimanded.

Mothman across the table, a pretzel of dark flesh, staring at him with the technologized eyes, speaking to him with the static grin. Mirrors everywhere.

History of mothmen as imploded hubs of electrical impulses, or memories that have escaped technorganic confinement and congealed into angry insect sphincters. Tracking shot of the Côte d'Azur . . . dragracing across the Mediterranean . . . one blue port after another, masts and lighthouses and basilicas and hoteltops . . .

Accelerando.

They incorporated Curd's noctural, chitinous experiences into the soap opera. Eventually they ran out of ideas and incorporated all of his experiences, real and imagined, "human" and "inhuman." Meanwhile Curd wallowed in ignorance and fame. Inevitably the government commandeered Panthermodern Enterprises, the production company of *The Idaho Reality*, with the sole intention of weaponizing Curd. They didn't know how specifically he might be weaponized since they didn't know much about mothmen, which lingered more in the realm of fiction than fact. The force of the actor's ego alone, however, if properly harnessed, might function as a capable means of total annihilation. It was agreed. Veins were opened and requisite palms were greased with blood/money. In time everybody's worst fears were accomplished.

Then: raucous cheers and rancorous parades.

Deft Characterization

Inside the actor's studio, Curd lit a rollie with a match, leaned forward in his chair, and delivered a powerful crowdstare to the audience. "Let me tell you how I negotiate the role of Seneca Beaulac," he said, eyes obscenely overweight and decisive. "It's a secret. But some secrets are meant to be secreted."

Blinking, he slouched backwards and looked at the host of the show, the spitting effigy of his father before the War. And the onset of adulthood.

Traumnovelle

Curd placed the ribbed carapace against his cheek and said, "Things are getting weirder. Not sure what to do at this point. I feel . . . I don't know what I feel. I feel unholy. Unmarketable. Membranous."

"Idaho," said a voice on the other end of the line.

"I think I might be a mothman. But nobody's telling me the truth."

Dead air. Dial tone. Static. Automated voice.

Liminality.

He observed the colored leaves of autumn spread upon the grass and then retired to the closest vanity mirror.

Discomfort. Eyelash on his eyeball.

No—something else.

He pulled the eyelid aside like a curtain and inspected the terrain beneath the arid folds of skin.

There it was.

He used tweezers to remove it, disavowing the torque of his brain matter as it seemed to swivel within his skullbone like a broken Lazy Susan. It must have been in there for years. It looked like a dirty pipe cleaner, twice doubled over. Amazing.

He dashed to the Orange Bathroom, long and thin and foreboding, and showed his mother. Horrified, she denied it, clutching together the lapels of her robe as she backed into a demolished shower stall. It wasn't a hair after all. He inspected the unit and assured her that some portion of it was indeed hairlike. Mother began to yank on her tongue. He tried to stop her, wingtips twitching in consternation, eyes aglow. But it was too late. That story was over . . .

Deep in the hull of the *S.S. Misanthrope*, a hirsute ur-man escaped from a window in Time and, bewildered, staggered towards him like a drunken synthespian. Curd dashed upstairs and leapt outside. Blinding blue sky. He seized a long metal pole from the flybridge and hurled it over his shoulder.

The ur-man's buttersoft flesh suffered a mortal blow. A Jelly Result preceded the clank of iron curtains.

Ad Lib

Lately, accusations fell on the use of a curious appendage
to dialogue that regarded selfhood and the chronic asser-
tion of identity and individuality. Here is the appendage:
". . . the likes of which the world has never seen."

The Bureau of Me

"I can't live without you anymore," said Hannah Harcourt, taking him by the wrist. "Please. I love you. I need you." She pushed together her elbows and produced cleavage.

Chestpiece of a stethoscope tossed over his shoulder, Dr. Seneca Beaulac gripped the lapels of a stiff, starched lab jacket and looked her up and down, disgusted, as if she were a fresh burn victim. "Fuck you, asshole," he said after a long silence. "I haven't seen you in, like, twenty years. *Exactly* twenty years, in fact. You left me. Remember? Skank. Suddenly you show up and want a dick? Fuck you! Period."

[It isn't in the script. Nothing he says is in the script anymore. But at this point the director knows better than to interrupt. He can always dub and surrogate the scene and bribe Curd's lawyers down the line. If he can help it, he won't end up like the last six directors, nameless and blackballed, skidrowed at Curd's sadistic whimsy. In the end, the player always wins.]

Harcourt's cleavageline disappeared like seams yanked out of fabric. She stepped backwards, wounded, despite the verity of Beaulac's claim, despite being married, many times, and in love, many times, with many other men, sometimes multiple men at the same time, but every time her suitors left her, one at time, unable to tolerate the persona, the mania.

There was also the issue of narrative deviation.

Beaulac sighed heavily and rolled his eyes. He put the bowl of a palm to his mouth. "Hey asshole!" he exclaimed. "Hey fuckhead! Can't we just do a 1980s slasher thing? Jesus! For once I'd like to fucking kill somebody! Somebody give me a machete and a fucked-up face! I'm sick of railing broads! I'd rather hack 'em up, fucker! Fuckin' dumbass!"

[The director flinches in the crow's nest, slumps deeper into his seat. Curd is talking to him. Maybe if he just pretends otherwise things will work themselves out? Maybe Curd's dialogue will somehow thread into the prescribed watercourse of the soapoperative? The onus was on Hannah Harcourt now. Could this idle bimbo parry the scatbombs of his word horde? More than that, could she make sense of them, i.e., could she convey to the audience that they were purposeful words, deliberate words, words worthy of sense and sensibility? Better if Curd just lifted up her dress and fucked her in the ass.]

Beaulac gripped Harcourt firmly by the shoulder, spun her around and pushed her over a reception desk. He pushed her too hard and she slid across the desk and pencils and pens and papers scattered everywhere. Stout, lineless nurses ducked out of the way as Beaulac ripped open his jacket—buttons flying—and hurdled the desk. He yanked Harcourt off the floor and cradled her in his arms in such a way that bystanders couldn't tell if he was going to strangle or kiss her; everyone on the set froze in place and looked on expectantly, waiting to see what would happen as hungry cameras moved in from the four corners of the ceiling on trackless tracking devices. Abruptly the scene slipped into sheer metaphor. She parted the lips of her consciousness in an effort to address the issue, but he clutched her selfhood, and desire spilled from the technologies that irised open on the industrial underbelly of her mind. Constellation of pulsing cyphers. Theme songs ejaculated into the afternoon. Wind. The leaves rustled, at first, then lay still, hanging from the branches like moist washcloths. They vaporized as a tornado the size of Ohio ripped across the ass-end of Idaho. Cameras imploded like realities. Closeup on a viole(n)t objective. At that moment it occurred to Dr. Seneca Beaulac that the name of the scene should be "The Viole(n)t Objective." Curd disagreed, preferring something more accessible, tenable, and above all, serious. He was a serious man, after all, and these were serious circumstances. He would not allow this character to drag him into the pit of absurdity and meaninglessness, in spite of the degree to which certain hirsute geographies would evade him, given world enough, and time.

[Bald and bearded, the executive producer storms the crow's nest like a deranged grizzly, moving forward as if pulled by a string attached to his Adam's apple. "This is getting bad," the director informs him. "I'm not sure what to do at this point." The executive producer reprimands him sternly and presents several options, among them a viole(n)t objective . . .]

Back in the Idaho Reality . . .

[Three "synthespians" crash the set and "dogmatize" how Occam's Razor hacked them like "geostationary quartz-stones" from the woodblock of a "Bureau of Me."

SENECA BEAULAC
(deadpan)
Me. That sounds familiar.

The executive producer, the director, and vast teams of overpaid, unwarranted writers rifle through the script in search of a potential hit. Something about what Curd said sounds familiar.

The "synthespians" wear jetblack "plainsuits" and "plainties" and they don't have irises; pupils dance across spheres of "white fire" as they scan the room. One of them lifts an arm and points at the sign around Beaulac's neck:

CLOTHES
CLOTHES
MORE CLOTHES

He lowers the arm and then all three of them converge on Beaulac and attempt to stuff him into a large dufflebag.]

Back to the Idaho Reality. Back to the Idaho Reality. Back to the Idaho Reality . . .

[The "synthespians" collectively "gesticulate" in a way that produces an "abracadabra effekt."

Hannah Harcourt begins to play with herself. This offsets everybody, even the "synthespians," one of whom "disavows the obscenity" with an "alien shriek" that reminds several listeners of a "tsunami of moths." Beaulac punches the "synthespian," silencing him, then slaps Harcourt, stunning her. The "synthespian"'s shirt comes loose and exposes a partially muscled skeleton. A terrific brawl ensues. Sometimes the superstylized fight sequences flashcut into graphic Roman orgies á la *Caligula*. Viewers and participants can't discern whether or not the flashcuts are real, i.e., if they are happening within the diegesis of the *The Idaho Reality* (and thus generated by revolutionary special effects techniques) or the result of some spectral anomaly. Everybody begins to doubt everything, all of it semantic, ranging from the meaning of fleeting glances to the meaning of existence and the cosmos. The episode spirals into Molten Discharge by the time the police show up and flog whoever gets in their way. "Administration" called the cops and they have been told that Curd started it all. But he has retreated to the walls, the ceiling. With "beaklike" arms and legs he "scurries like a vermin" across "acausal regions" and there's nothing anybody can do to stop him . . .]

Soliloquy to Gods & Men

"I may not belong to physical reality. I may not possess an elastic core. I may not ascribe rational denovations to the underarms of humanity. But I have spoken to cockroaches in the dark. If nothing else, I promise you a Cult of Personality the likes of which the world has never seen," intoned Curd, voice resounding over the roofs of the world. "At any rate, there I was, in Idaho, after being sidetracked for days in Wall, South Dakota. I yearned for a wet slut, but the desert infects bodies as much as it does minds, souls, and other etherealities. Unexpectedly a slue of drunken bikers accosted me in the Drug Store. I had done nothing to provoke the fuckers. But they seemed certain of themselves (i.e., certain of my culpability) and a long chase ensued atop loud motorcycles, one of which I confiscated so as to facilitate the drama that they had so ignominiously engendered. We blasted up and down the streets of Wall for hours scaring away natives and tourists in equal measure. *Ennui* greeted me like an abused foster parent and I made the decision to total the vehicle. I veered wildly to the left and accelerated into an unimportant-looking building, destroying the motherfucker. I was ok. Completely unscathed, in fact, notwithstanding screwball backflips and earthshattering breakfalls. I might have lost consciousness, but the loss of consciousness is such a mundane affair, it need not be mentioned; I slept last night, and I will sleep tonight, snoring like a fat baconwhore. I must say the reality of this state violates certain hauntological codes, but the landscape is sound, and that's why I'm here. Idaho is more earthlike than earth itself. I wish you could see it—the way the social fabric peels apart to expose such gristled cloak-and-dagger mechanisms, not to mention the centrifugal eccentricity, the subterranean implosion, the dismantling narratives of Shit and Truth. I can assure you that this interzone is spud-free. Canny subjects embrace the covenant. It's a matter of angles of incidence. These angles constitute humanity. The gods rob me of my godlessness. As always, I forgive them; but I never forget a fuckin' asshole. I once went to a drive-in movie conscious of the fact that it was high noon and the projectionist was asleep. Try it. Try to sit there, in your car, in the dust, staring at the blank megascreen. You will fail. Eventually everybody fails. The recalcitrant ethics of mindlessness delude us into believing that we actually possess selfhood and the capacity for violence.

But I can assure you: we lack selfhood. And we lack the capacity to exert violence. Violence exerts us. In the absence of fame, one ceases to exist. I might play Seneca Beaulac on TV, but in reality, I am an island, beachfronts groping in every direction for the Split Ends of Time. No man is an island, however, who fails to admit the great and powerful depth of his flaws. And yet, despite my flaws, and my limitations, and my unrealized dreams, and my blundered second-guesses and off-the-cuff glances, and so forth, despite these things, despite *me*, you stupid fuckheads, I can assure you of one thing: nobody—and I mean *nobody*, dead or undead, alive or moribund, not-yet-conceived or never-to-be-birthed—NOBODY CAN FUCK WITH MY MUSE."

Left Turn Signal

This is the last chapter of the book's bleeding heart, ventricles unhinged, lifeforce flowing into the copper-plated gutters. I'm following Curd in a Hepburn orange 1973 Buick Riviera. 3,000 miles and counting.

Curd's driving a motorcycle.

I can't tell what kind.

Handlebars like elkhorns—he can barely reach them, maneuver them.

At some point his left turn signal blinks on. There are no side roads. The main road goes on and on and there's nothing but beanfields to the east and to the west and anybody in this situation can only think and dream of asphalt and beans and sky.

He keeps the turn signal on for a long time. At last he jerks left. Plunges into the beanfield.

I pull to the roadside, get out of the car.

I stand on my toes, sensing the curvature of my calf muscles, and watch him go.

He goes on and on and when I can barely see him he wipes out, awkwardly, like a child who doesn't know the score. A plume of dust climbs into the blue rafters.

ABOUT THE AUTHOR

D. HARLAN WILSON is an award-winning, critically acclaimed novelist, short fiction writer, theorist, editor, historian, publisher and English prof. Visit him online at **DHarlanWilson.com** and **TheKyotoMan.com**.

90739690R00071

Made in the USA
Middletown, DE
26 September 2018